Dear mouse friends,
Welcome to the world of

Geronimo Stilton

Geronimo Stilton
A learned and brainy
mouse; editor of
The Rodent's Gazette

Thea Stilton
Geronimo's sister and
special correspondent at
The Rodent's Gazette

Trap Stilton
An awful joker;
Geronimo's cousin and
owner of the store
Cheap Junk for Less

Benjamin Stilton
A sweet and loving
nine-year-old mouse;
Geronimo's favorite
nephew

Geronimo Stilton

TREASURES
OF THE MAYA

Scholastic Inc.

Copyright © 2020 by Edizioni Piemme S.p.A., Palazzo Mondadori, Via Mondadori 1, 20090 Segrate, Italy. International Rights © Atlantyca S.p.A. English translation © 2023 by Atlantyca S.p.A.

The publisher does not have any control over and does not assume any responsibility for author or third-party websites or their content.

GERONIMO STILTON names, characters, and related indicia are copyright, trademark, and exclusive license of Atlantyca S.p.A. All rights reserved. The moral right of the author has been asserted. Based on an original idea by Elisabetta Dami. geronimostilton.com

Published by Scholastic Inc., *Publishers since 1920*, 557 Broadway, New York, NY 10012. SCHOLASTIC and associated logos are trademarks and/or registered trademarks of Scholastic Inc.

Stilton is the name of a famous English cheese. It is a registered trademark of the Stilton Cheesemakers' Association.

No part of this publication may be reproduced, stored in a retrieval system, or transmitted in any form or by any means, electronic, mechanical, photocopying, recording, or otherwise, without written permission of the copyright holder. For information regarding permission, please contact: Atlantyca S.p.A., Corso Magenta 60/62, 20123 Milan, Italy; e-mail foreignrights@atlantyca.it, atlantyca.com.

This book is a work of fiction. Names, characters, places, and incidents are either the product of the author's imagination or are used fictitiously, and any resemblance to actual persons, living or dead, business establishments, events, or locales is entirely coincidental.

ISBN 978-1-339-02769-2

Text by Geronimo Stilton
Original title *Il Tesoro dei maya*

Art director: Iacopo Bruno
Cover by Guiseppe Facciotto and Christian Aliprandi
Graphic Designer: Alice Iuri/theWorldofDOT
Illustrations by Guiseppe Facciotto, Carolina Livio, Daria Cherchi, and Valeria Cairoli
Translated by Anna Pizzelli
Special thanks to Anna Bloom
Interior design by Becky James

10 9 8 7 6 5 4 3 2 1   24 25 26 27 28

Printed in China   38
First printing 2024

BEEP, BEEP, BEEP!

I remember that Sunday morning **very** well.

There I was, happily **snoring** under my blankets, just like I do every Sunday morning, when the *strangest* thing happened —

But wait! I forgot to introduce myself. My name is Stilton, *Geronimo Stilton*, and I am the editor in chief of *The Rodent's Gazette*, the most **famouse** newspaper on Mouse Island.

Like I was saying, I was sleeping **peacefully** until a sudden **shrieking** sound woke me up!

BEEP, BEEP, BEEP!

It was the sound of some kind of **ALARM!**

"**Squeak!**" I shouted. I sat up in bed, looking everywhere for the source of the noise. It wasn't my regular **ALARM** clock or my phone. "What could it be?"

Suddenly, I remembered. That **LOUD** sound was coming from my *fancy* new computer. It had been specially built for me by my friend Beaker Poirat.

I needed to turn it off quickly. The sound was so loud the windows were shaking like mozzarella pudding!

I threw off my blankets and struggled to get out of bed. But the ALARM shook the walls so much, the bookcase above my head started to come free from the wall.

A **heavy** book toppled over and landed right on my snout. "Rancid ricotta!" I cried, rubbing the spot where a bump was rapidly forming.

I lurched off the bed, tossing blankets and books to the ground. Now if I could only remember how to silence that ALARM. I stepped forward, determined to have quiet.

Just then a GUST of wind rattled the

side of the house. My bedroom window flew open. The curtains swirled all around me. I couldn't see anything!

"Holey Swiss cheese!" I yelled, while batting the curtains all around.

"This is worse than that time I fell into the vat of FONDUE!"

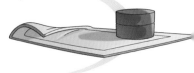

I finally escaped the curtains . . . only to trip on the carpet and SPLAT on the floor like a cheesy meatball rolling off a table.

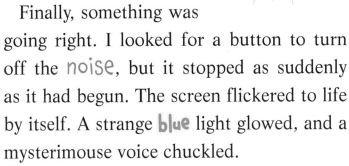

I had landed on my tail, exactly in front of my computer!

Finally, something was going right. I looked for a button to turn off the noise, but it stopped as suddenly as it had begun. The screen flickered to life by itself. A strange blue light glowed, and a mysterimouse voice chuckled.

"Geronimo, you stinky cheese — how did you like my trick?"

4.

I TRIPPED ON THE CARPET . . .

5.

AND TOOK A SCARY TUMBLE . . .

6.

BUT I LANDED ON MY TAIL RIGHT IN FRONT OF THE COMPUTER.

THE COMPUTER

It is a prototype put together for Geronimo by his friend Beaker Poirat. His real name is **C35829XTPQRIIO**, but it is much easier to just call him **COMPUTER**.

STATS:

1. Computer is pistachio green, which is Beaker's favorite color.

2. He's completely eco-friendly, made of recycled plastic mixed with lots and lots of pistachio shells.

3. He is powered by a long-lasting battery made with fermented pistachio pulp — he can run for a year without being charged!

4. A special microchip allows Computer to behave like a real robot. For example, he can speak all the languages in the world, he can drive a car when properly connected to it, and he can even order pizza! He keeps track of Geronimo's to-do list and is very good at telling jokes. (He loves to play tricks on Geronimo.)

5. He has two mechanical arms.

WARNING: Since Computer is only a prototype, he has not been perfected yet. His feelings are easily hurt, and when that happens, he pouts and shuts himself off.

I have a lot of special functions: I can drive, order anything you want, remind you of tasks you need to accomplish, crack jokes, play tricks, and I also know all the recipes in the world.

Have you heard the latest cheese joke? I am an expert and know them all! Go ahead, ask me.

Every once in a while, my feelings get hurt. I am not fond of bad manners.

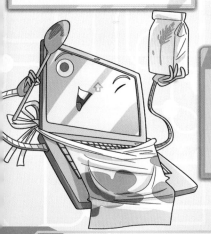

Cooking is an art, and I am a real professional. You don't believe me? Try my cookies!

A REAL SCAREDY-MOUSE!

I crawled over to Computer, shaking my snout. "You are a real **prankster**!"

The computer giggled. "Hee, hee, hee. That was a great trick, don't you think? You should have seen your scaredy snout when the **ALARM** went off!"

I ROLLED my eyes. "Ha, ha, very **funny**. But now could you do your job? Do I have any new messages?"

Computer **frowned**. "Fine! Let's see — you have one email from your CHEESE OF THE MONTH

CLUB, one from your nephew, and one from your sister, Thea." The screen flashed. "It looks urgent. You better read the one from Thea first."

I went to scroll through my inbox, but Computer moved the cursor away from me. "I could read it to you?" he asked.

"Absolutely not," I said. "I'm quite capable of reading my own emails. Especially now that I'm WIDE-AWAKE." I gave the computer a pointed stare.

"I was only trying to help!" Computer SNAPPED. "Fine, do it yourself, you cheddarhead! Good-bye!" With that, the computer's cartoon avatar winked out, leaving me alone.

So sensitive!

I sighed. I hadn't meant to hurt his

feelings, but I was happy to have some quiet.

I clicked over to Thea's email and began to read. I turned as pale as a piece of MOZZARELLA when I saw what she had written.

From: Thea Stilton
To: Geronimo Stilton
Dear Brother,
I went on a secret mission to the Chichén Itzá archaeological site in México's Yucatán Peninsula. But now I find myself in danger! Please come as soon as possible to help me. I am at a place called the Mobile Mouseum

What???

The message just ended in the middle of a sentence! It looked like she'd been interrupted and had to hit send without finishing her email. I remembered from my previous travels that Chichén Itzá was **famouse** for its ancient Maya ruins featuring incredimouse stone pyramids.

Why had my SISTER gone to Chichén Itzá? And why was she now in DANGER?

TIME FOR A TRIP!

Computer's avatar suddenly returned. "Thea is in DANGER? Oh no!"

My whiskers trembled. "I don't have time for any of your tricks right now. I need to get to México as quickly as possible!"

Computer started BEEPING and blinking. Different browser windows popped up. "Don't be a worryrat, Geronimo! This is my time to shine!"

As I watched, he scrolled through discount ticket websites, car service pages, and weather reports.

All the while, he mumbled to himself. "Chichén Itzá . . . Cancún is the closest airport. Let's get you a tourist visa . . . and

VISA

a plane ticket. Here is the packing list for your suitcase based on the current temperature . . . Then I will book you a car . . .

Now to **search** for info on the Mobile Mouseum . . ."

Wow! This was *FASTER*

TICKET

and better than I could have done myself!

SUITCASES

"I am sorry I was rude. Thank you!"

TAXI

Computer BEEPED. "I'm happy to do it!"

"I almost wish you could come to México with me," I said, smiling. Computer had been pretty helpful . . . this time.

"Oh, I am coming!" Computer chirped. "I have your e-ticket — you have to bring me. We're going to have so much **fun**!"

I groaned. "Fine. But you have to promise to behave yourself! Thea is in trouble. This isn't just some vacation — this is serious!"

"I promise to behave," Computer said. "You will not regret this, Geronimo!"

Thanks to Computer's packing list, I was ready to go in twenty minutes. The car he had ordered picked me up promptly, so we were at the airport in plenty of time for our flight.

Once I boarded the plane and walked to my seat, I was shocked to see two rodents I knew very well. My best friends Bruce Hyena and Hercule Poirat!

"What are you two cheese sticks doing here?" I asked.

They both looked confused. "You silly Swiss cheese," Poirat said. "You invited us!"

"Yeah!" Bruce chimed in. "Don't you remember? You sent us an email this morning and said it was an **EMERGENCY**! We needed to come to México with you today to rescue Thea."

I stared at them, my snout dropping open. Then I realized what had happened. I pulled

What are you doing here?

Sit down, Geronimo!

Computer out of my bag. "Did you do this?" I asked.

Computer looked a little embarrassed. "Well, I did, actually. I thought you might need help. Sometimes you can be kind of a scaredy-mouse."

Well, he wasn't totally **WRONG** about that — not that I wanted to admit it! But before I could say anything, the flight attendants started to close the cabin door. I took my seat.

As the plane took off, I thought about Thea's message and tried to stay **calm**. I'd need to have a CLEAR mind to help her.

What had she been doing at the Mobile Mouseum in Chichén Itzá? To distract myself, I started **reading** a very interesting archaeology magazine.

Unfortunately, it was hard to concentrate

because my travel companions started **ARGUING**.

"I will be the biggest help to Thea," Bruce **bragged**. "No doubt about it."

MAYA

THEFT!

A ruthless jewelry collector has been arranging the theft of precious antique jewelry all over the world. The thief's biggest passion is Maya jewelry . . .

Poirat shook his snout. "I am the **WORLD'S GREATEST** detective!" he cried. "I will of course be the most helpful."

"I will help Thea the **most**!"

"No, I will help her the **most**!"

"No, I will!"

"I said I will!"

"I will, I will!"

"I willllllll!"

I put my paws over my ears. Even Computer got fed up. "Enough, both of you!" he beeped. "Before anymouse can help Thea, we need to do some **RESEARCH**. I will now read you what I've found out about Mexico!"

MÉXICO

LOCATION: Central America. Shares a northern border with the United States. In the southeast, it borders Guatemala and Belize.

CAPITAL: México City

LANGUAGE: Spanish

CURRENCY: Méxican peso

HISTORY: Humans have lived in what is now México for about 20,000 years. Among the best known pre-Columbian civilizations is the Olmec, who lived in southern México. Later, other groups rose to prominence, like the Zapotec, Maya, and Teotihuacán civilizations. When Spanish colonizers arrived in the 1500s, the Aztecs controlled a large area of central México.

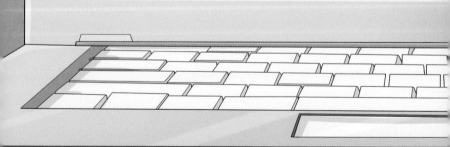

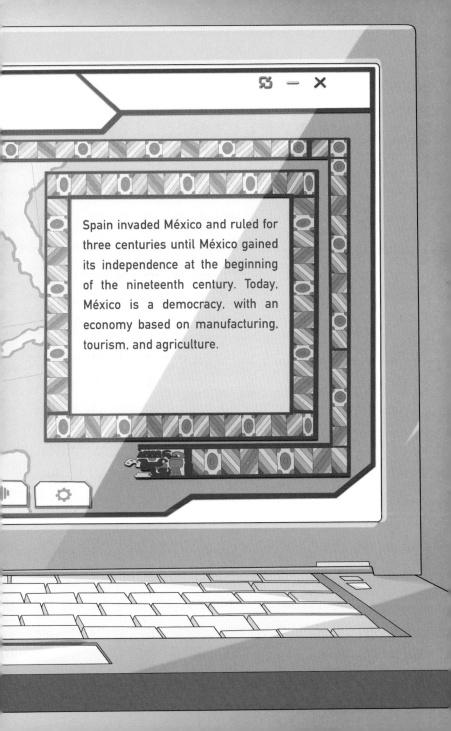

Spain invaded México and ruled for three centuries until México gained its independence at the beginning of the nineteenth century. Today, México is a democracy, with an economy based on manufacturing, tourism, and agriculture.

WELCOME TO MÉXICO!

After a long flight, the airplane finally landed at the Cancún airport, in México's Yucatán Peninsula.

Computer started taking pictures nonstop.

Flash, flash, flash!

"Did you know I can take incredimouse pictures, Geronimo? Did you also know that I am fluent in every language in the world? *Welcome* in Spanish is *bienvenido*."

Computer was obviously excited, but for me, this was no vacation. I needed to find Thea!

I had sent her an email with my flight

info. Part of me had been hoping she'd be here waiting, but there was no sign of her. I hoped she was okay!

Just then someone called out in Spanish: "*¿Señor Geronimo?*"

I turned around to see a red-haired rodent wearing a blue jacket. "Yes, my name is Stilton, *Geronimo Stilton*!"

¿Señor Geronimo?

OSCAR RATON
MOBILE MOUSEUM DIRECTOR

CAREER:

Ever since he was a young mouse, Oscar dreamed of becoming an archaeologist. He was really smart. By the time he was three, he was already attending elementary school, by eight he was in middle school, and by the time he was thirteen, he was in college!

He now holds a master's degree in archaeology and has written many books on the history of ancient civilizations.

Currently, he is the director of the Mobile Mouseum, a branch of the Archaeology Institute on Mouse Island. Every week, he hosts a popular TV show called *The Maya Experience*.

HIS PASSIONS:

Music: He can play any traditional Mexican song with his guitar!

Cooking: He is an expert in Mexican cuisine.

Gardening: He grows jalapeño peppers behind the Mobile Mouseum, which he then uses in his recipes.

His dream: He would love to travel the world with his Mobile Mouseum to share his archaeological adventures and his love of Mexican cuisine.

The rodent shook my paw. "Bienvenido, *yo soy* Oscar Raton. I am the director of the Mobile Mouseum, a branch of the Archaeology Institute of Mouse Island. Every week, I film an episode of *The Maya Experience* here. Perhaps you have seen it?"

From behind me, I heard:

Flash, flash, flash!

Computer let out a Squeal as he snapped more pictures. "Of course we've heard of your show! I've seen every episode!"

Oscar smiled at Computer before continuing. "A friend of yours from the Mouse Island Egyptian Mouseum advised me of your arrival, so I came to **greet** you myself."

My snout fell open in SURPRISE. "But how did the professor know I was coming? I left in a *RUSH*."

Computer's screen blushed. "Well . . . that was me. I told the professor about our trip, so I could request access to his database on ancient civilizations. That's how I was so well prepared when I talked to you on the PLANE. I didn't think you'd mind."

Oscar wrinkled his snout. "I hope it's okay I'm here. I hired your sister, Thea, when I first found the Maya treasure.* I know she is a very talented photographer."

I nodded. "Of course. Thea is Mouse Island's most FABUMOUSE photographer, a superb special correspondent, and a brave mouse."

Oscar looked solemn. "Well, yes. But now

* The Maya treasure Oscar discovered is a gold chest containing a fourteen-carat gold necklace, with a pendant in the shape of the sun.

I'm **SORRY** I ever asked Thea to come. I can't find her anywhere! We were meeting this morning, but she **disappeared**. When I heard you were coming, I wanted to squeak to you as soon as possible."

My heart sank. I had suspected something had happened to Thea when I got her STRANGE email, but Oscar had just confirmed it — Thea was **MISSING**.

"That's not all," Oscar continued. "The treasure is gone as well. I need your help!"

Bruce let out a

THEA STILTON

NAME: Thea Stilton

JOB: Special correspondent for *The Rodent's Gazette*

PASSIONS: She loves traveling and adventures. She is a nature photographer and likes to write about cultural and current events. When Oscar contacted her about a Maya treasure, she immediately took off for Cancún.

squeak, and Poirat's whiskers trembled.

Poirat nervously twisted his paws together. "We must find her — at once!"

"Don't PANIC; I will find her," Bruce said.

"No, I will!" Poirat cried.

Computer let out a series of short, loud beeps to silence them.

BEEP, BEEP, BEEEEP!

I nodded to him in thanks. "We will all need to work together to find Thea and help her out of whatever trouble she's in. Teamwork is the only way. It's what Thea would want," I added sternly.

Poirat and Bruce looked apologetic.

"Sorry, Geronimo," they said together.

"I'm sorry, too!" Oscar said. "For getting Thea into trouble in the first place!" He burst into tears, which made the other two cry as well. They shared a hug as I stood off to the side and ROLLED my eyes.

"Thea would also want us to hurry," I said. "Let's get going!"

Oscar wiped his eyes, scooped up some of our luggage, and pointed the way toward a waiting van. "This way — let's get Operation: Rescue Thea started!"

WELCOME TO
CHICHÉN ITZÁ!

We drove directly to the Chichén Itzá archaeological site. There, Oscar took us into the area where his Mobile Mouseum

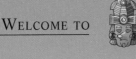

was located, thanks to a special permit.

He sighed **dreamily**. "There is the Chichén Itzá pyramid. Doesn't it just take your breath away?"

Squeak, amazing!

Computer started **shaking** his screen with excitement. He began taking pictures nonstop.

What a sight!

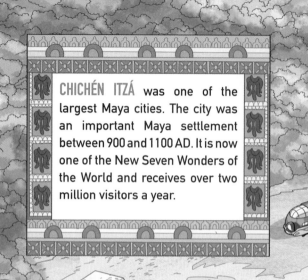

CHICHÉN ITZÁ was one of the largest Maya cities. The city was an important Maya settlement between 900 and 1100 AD. It is now one of the New Seven Wonders of the World and receives over two million visitors a year.

LEGEND:

1. Observatory or El Caracol
2. Tomb of the Great Priest and Ossuary
3. Temple of the Jaguar and ballgame court
4. The Platform of the Eagles and Jaguars
5. The Venus Platform or Temple of Venus
6. Pyramid of Kukulán or El Castillo
7. Court of a Thousand Columns and the Temple of the Warriors

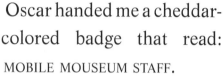

Oscar handed me a cheddar-colored badge that read: MOBILE MOUSEUM STAFF.

Computer let out a low, **sad** beep. "No badge for the poor little computer?" he asked. Slowly, the laptop screen descended as he closed up like a **CLAMSHELL**.

Oscar looked at me, but I just **shrugged**. "Um, let me see

here," Oscar said. I could see him scanning around for something to make Computer feel better. He  saw a sheet of program **STICKERS** and his eyes lit up. "Ah, here we are! The special

Electronic Guest badge."
He attached a sticker to
the top of Computer. "You
are part of the team!"

Computer immediately woke up and let
out a series of cheerful beeps. "Why, yes,
I am. I am the most VALUABLE member of
the team!"

"Just let him have it," I **WHISPERED** to a
confused-looking Oscar.

Oscar handed Bruce and Poirat their
badges. Now that we were all official,
Oscar walked us to the Mobile Mouseum.
We finally understood why it was called
that: The mouseum was not a building but
a **VEHICLE**, sort of like a very big, fancy
camper van.

THE MAYA EXPERIENCE was written across
the front of the mouseum and huge TV

antennae sprouted from the top.

"This camper is very well equipped to stream our program, *The Maya Experience*. Even though it's **smaller** than a real TV studio, we have all the latest state-of-the-art equipment. We can stream anywhere in the world, right from here."

"We are moving to another location soon," Oscar continued. "But I can't tell you where. That's under wraps for now."

Wow!

Here is the Mobile Mouseum!

I frowned. "We wouldn't mention it to any other rodents."

"I know," Oscar said. "But I promised I would keep it a **SECRET**! I can tell you this fun fact — the Mobile Mouseum was built by the famouse genius and inventor Professor Beaker Poirat."

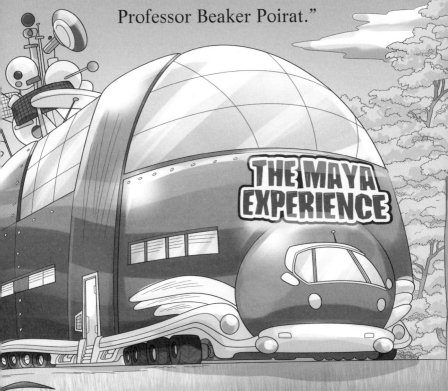

"I am **good** friends with Beaker," I said. "In fact —" But before I could finish, Computer let out an excited **BEEP**.

"Beaker is a real genius. I know because he invented **ME**!" Computer looked smug for a moment, but then his expression changed. "Wait a minute! I'm detecting a signal from Thea's cell phone! She is right *here*, in the Mobile Mouseum!"

"Are you sure?" I asked, excited.

Oscar shook his snout **sadly**. "I'm afraid that's impawssible. Thea has not been seen since the Maya treasure disappeared!"

Computer BEEPED stubbornly. "We should go inside and search!"

Oscar shrugged. "We can. But as you can see, it's not a **GIANT** mouseum."

Just then the Mobile Mouseum door swung open and the smell of eucalyptus washed over us. I glanced over, half hoping to see Thea. But it wasn't her. Standing there instead was a gruff-looking ratlet, **chomping** on gum. And he was staring right at me!

A MYSTERIMOUSE RAT!

That mysterimouse rat was very **TALL** and strong. His outfit made him seem like he was ready for any kind of adventure.

He was wearing a ripped khaki shirt and matching pants, with an **ORANGE** linen scarf that had initials stitched on it. He was also wearing a belt with various tools hanging off it, but one of the hooks was empty. A wide-brimmed hat shaded his snout, and dark sunglasses hid his eyes.

"*Buenos días.* Yo soy Manny Chego."

Oscar introduced all of us **one** by **one**.

"And this is Geronimo Stilton," he finished, pointing a paw in my direction.

Manny's eyes FLASHED. His snout curled up like he smelled rotten cheese. "Ah, you are the famouse Geronimo Stilton, Thea's brother?"

"Yes, that's me," I said. I put out my paw to shake, but Manny just continued to stare at me.

"Thea Stilton is the moldy cheese who made off with the Maya treasure. She should be ashamed of herself!"

Anger bubbled up in me like boiling fondue. "How dare you!" I yelled. "My sister, Thea, is an honest mouse! She would never steal anything, let alone an important artifact!"

Bruce Hyena scowled. "Thea is missing and could be in trouble."

"How do we know one of you RATS didn't steal the treasure and frame Thea?"

Poirat asked. He looked first at Manny and then Oscar.

A look of shock came over Oscar's snout. "I have never stolen anything!"

Computer began to snap pictures of Manny. I could hear him mumbling: "I really do not like the **stink** of this cheese . . ."

Personally, I had to agree, so I didn't tell Computer to stop. Maybe the photos would be useful later.

Manny sneered at Computer. "Oscar, I will leave you to your guests. I am going to town to buy a new compass. I will be back this evening. *¡Adiós!*" He **STOMPED** off.

"Who is that grumpy Gouda?" Poirat asked.

Oscar sighed. "Manny is a documentary filmmaker who specializes in ancient civilizations. He's been collaborating with me for about a month on a new project, a movie about the Maya. He is very talented but a little difficult sometimes. I apologize for what he said. I don't agree with him at all, but the necklace did disappear when Thea arrived, so I can see how his suspicions got started."

"Why don't you tell us what happened?" I suggested.

OSCAR'S STORY:

1. About a week ago while I was walking behind the main Chichén Itzá pyramid, I tripped over something sticking up out of the mud. It was a gold chest. Inside it was an incredimouse gold necklace!

2. I notified the authorities and they asked me to study the treasure. Then I hired Thea Stilton to come take some photos for me.

3. I showed Thea the necklace, which was stored in a safe area of the Mobile Mouseum, where we keep the most precious artifacts.

4. Suddenly, the fire alarm went off. I ran outside to look for help, while Thea stayed behind.

I need your help. I must find the treasure, but I want to find Thea, too!

5. When I got back, Thea was gone . . . and so was the priceless Maya necklace!

6. Manny blamed me for everything and has publicly accused Thea of stealing the treasure.

WELCOME TO THE MOBILE MOUSEUM!

.

After his account of the facts, Oscar invited us inside. "Come, I will show you around. Maybe you will find a **clue** that I missed."

Our first stop was his office (1), furnished with old wooden furniture. A lot of certificates hung on the walls. He noticed Bruce looking at them. "I've won a number of AWARDS for my archaeological work."

Poirat took it all in. "You must be one smart slice of cheese," he said. I couldn't tell if he was kidding, but Oscar looked pleased.

In the Maya Artifacts Hall

(2), there were a number of objects displayed, each one with an explanation card. "This is all very **impressive**," I said. For such a **small** mouseum, there was a lot to look at!

2

Bruce nudged me with his elbow. "We should all **cool** it on the compliments," he whispered. "I think he's got a big enough cheddarhead as it is."

Then we walked into the library (3), where books about the Maya civilization lined the shelves. They looked like they had been carefully organized.

3

Another hall housed the archives (4), where Oscar kept records of his own finds.

4

Then Oscar took us into a room

Mobile Mouseum

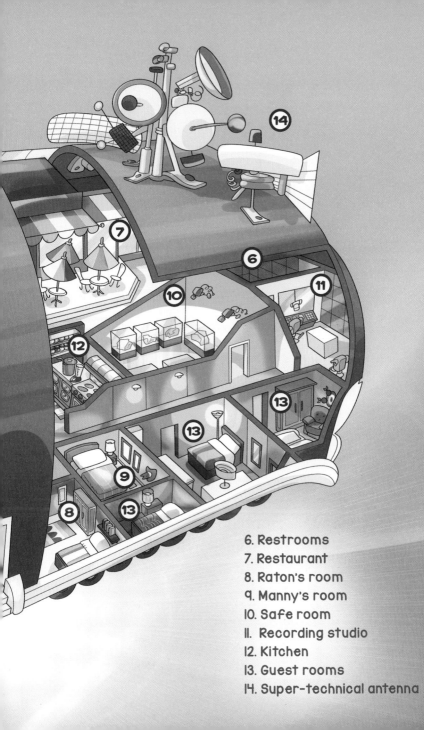

6. Restrooms
7. Restaurant
8. Raton's room
9. Manny's room
10. Safe room
11. Recording studio
12. Kitchen
13. Guest rooms
14. Super-technical antenna

where key rings, small statues, cards, **colorful** earthenware pots, and reproductions of Mexican pyramids were displayed. "This is our souvenir store (5)," he said.

The restrooms (6) were in a corner, which Oscar proudly showed us. "See how everything is CLEAN and neat? I personally check every detail so that everything always looks PERFECT!"

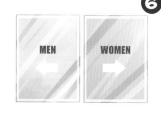

Suddenly, a delicious smell wafted across my snout. "Mmmm, what's that?" I asked. My stomach rumbled.

"This is our fabumouse cafeteria!" Oscar said, leading us into a new area (7). "We serve traditional Mexican dishes here."

He grabbed a taco from a nearby tray. "I helped prepare these tacos myself. I love cooking and my dream is to open a restaurant someday!"

Squeak! This was a mouse of many talents!

We each took a cheese-crusted fish taco and chomped happily in silence. For once, we could all agree on something — these were tasty! I took a second taco and turned to Oscar. "I can't believe what you've set up here."

Oscar looked wistful. "Thea said the exact same thing."

"We'll find her," I said. "Why don't you show us the room where you last saw Thea and the NECKLACE."

Oscar led the way through his room (8) and the room where

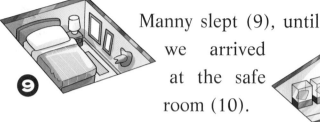

Manny slept (9), until we arrived at the safe room (10).

"This is where we store everything of value. This room is like a bank vault," Oscar said. "We kept the necklace here. This is the last place I saw Thea."

Bruce, Poirat, and I started to take a look around. Computer began taking nonstop photos. **Flash, flash, flash!**

Poirat pointed to a **CLOSED** door at the end of the hall. "Where does that lead to?" he asked.

"That room is the recording studio (11). That's where I stream my TV show. I spent a fortune soundproofing it with a special material that absorbs all sounds so

I don't get distracted while I record!"

Poirat wiggled the door handle, but the door was locked.

Oscar came over to check it himself. "Hmm. That's **weird** . . . why is it not opening?" He pulled his phone from his pocket. "Let me call Manny and see if he knows anything about it."

When he got off the phone, he came back over to us. "Manny says he noticed that the door was **STUCK** this morning. He called a locksmith, who is going to come by tomorrow."

Something about this locked door seemed STRANGE, but I couldn't quite put my paw on what it was. Oscar didn't seem bothered, so I decided not to be a worryrat about it. We had more pressing things to deal with — like finding Thea!

Hot Sauce Talk!

Oscar led us back to the restaurant kitchen. "You've come a **LONG** way and haven't eaten much. I'll make you a real meal, and then we can discuss next steps," he said.

Oscar busied himself getting out ingredients and utensils. Meanwhile, Computer continued to take endless pictures.

Flash, flash, flash!

"What are you doing?" I hissed.

Computer's screen displayed a pouting face. "You never know what could be a **clue**!" he said. Then his avatar stuck out his tongue at me.

I sighed and turned back to hear Oscar

talk about traditional Mexican cuisine. "Modern-day Mexican **FOOD** draws influence from Aztec and Maya traditions, as well as customs and ingredients introduced by Spanish colonizers. Beef and chicken are common proteins. Vegetables like broccoli, cauliflower, and radishes show up a lot as well. Mexican cuisine also uses a lot of **spices** and **peppers**, especially jalapeños."

Tacos

Whistling to himself, Oscar prepared another round of tacos. Then he started to scoop out avocados for guacamole.

Guacamole

He stirred a **LARGE** steaming pot. "This is a mixed **vegetable** stew, a simple dish with

Mixed vegetable stew

tomatoes, corn, carrots, beans, green beans, and lots more!" He ladled the stew into bowls for us.

Bruce inhaled deeply. "It smells great, Oscar! Where did you learn to cook like this?"

Oscar grinned. "My *abuela* taught me everything I know," he said. "I'm so glad I can share it with you all. Usually it's just me and Manny eating — and he's not much of a foodie!"

Poirat laughed. "It's hard to imagine him enjoying much of anything. He seemed very serious."

"Well, you got him on a **BAD** day," Oscar said. "He's very upset about the missing necklace."

Oscar presented us with another STEAMING dish. "These are *enchiladas rojas*. I filled corn tortillas with some chicken and topped them with my famouse red sauce, made with chiles I grow here at the Mobile Mouseum."

My stomach rumbled again. I couldn't wait to dig in!

Fajita

While we sampled the dishes, Oscar told us about some other popular foods of México. "Often we grill meat and fish, something we call **barbacoa**. Maybe I'll have a chance to make that for all of you once we find Thea and the necklace."

"That would be terrific!" I said.

"Another specialty of

Barbacoa

mine is garlic soup," Oscar said. "Here, try some. It's very good for you!"

Garlic soup

Oscar presented us with bowls of his soup. Poirat tasted his and smiled. "Geronimo, you must have some!" He fed me a SPOONFUL.

I swallowed carefully. I'm not much of an adventurous eater, but I didn't want

Beans

In México, as in other countries, beans are often served with rice. The two work together to form a complete vegetable protein. Beans themselves are a superfood: they contain fiber, potassium, folate, manganese, and magnesium.

to be rude. Hercule offered me some of his **BLACK** beans. "Try this. Beans have tons of protein and fiber — and taste delicious, too!"

Eat, Stilton!

Ha, ha!

Bruce Hyena grabbed a tortilla chip and zoomed it toward a bowl filled with salsa. "Yum!" he cried. "Spicy and fresh tasting. Here, Geronimo, you must try it!" He DIPPED a chip and handed it to me.

Slowly, I brought it toward my snout. "I

have a very low **heat** tolerance,"
I said. "Is it only a little spicy?"

Bruce nodded, so I took a **BIG**
bite.

Great gobs of flaming cheese!
This was the spiciest salsa I'd ever
tasted. My cheeks turned pink and
my eyes watered.

Bruce laughed as I frantically waved a paw
in front of my snout. "I guess it was pretty
spicy after all!" he said.

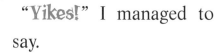

"Yikes!" I managed to
say.

Oscar dashed over.
"That was my super-
spicy salsa — not for salsa
newbies! Here, drink this
cheddar smoothie —
the dairy will help."

He handed me the **icy-cool** beverage, and I chugged gratefully. He was right. It helped a lot!

Computer started snapping pictures of me. "You should see what your snout looks like, Geronimo!"

I rubbed my whiskers, but Oscar nudged my elbow with his paw. "Careful not to touch your eyes. If you didn't like eating super-spicy salsa, you definitely don't want it in your eye!"

Squeak! I definitely didn't! I went to wash my paws. When I came back, Oscar had gotten out his work-in-progress cookbook to show Bruce and Poirat.

Guacamole

Ingredients:
Half a red onion
1 jalapeño pepper
1 small tomato
Cilantro
2 ripe avocados
Juice of half a lemon
Pinch of salt

Directions:
Ask an adult to help you! Slice the onion and the jalapeño in thin slices. Cut the tomato into small cubes. Chop the cilantro. Set aside. Cut the avocados in half, remove the pits, and scoop out the flesh. Mash the avocado in a bowl with a fork. Then mix in the ingredients that were set aside: onion, jalapeño, tomato, and cilantro. Add lemon juice and stir until blended. Add pinch of salt to taste.

La Cocada Candy

Ingredients:
5 cups of shredded coconut
4 cups of whole milk
3 cups of sugar
½ teaspoon of cinnamon
4 egg yolks
½ cup sliced almonds

Directions:
Ask an adult for help. In a pot, stir together shredded coconut, milk, sugar, and cinnamon. Cook mixture on a low flame until sugar is dissolved. Take off the

heat and let it sit for about 15 minutes. Then whisk in the egg yolks. Put back on the stove at medium heat until mixture thickens. Using a spoon, drop spoonfuls of the mixture onto parchment-lined cookie sheets. Sprinkle them with sliced almonds and place in the oven for 10 minutes.

Tomato Soup with Corn Tortillas

Ingredients:

5 ripe plum tomatoes
1 white onion
½ jalapeño pepper, seeds removed
4 tablespoons olive oil
Pinch of salt
3 cups chicken broth
15-16 corn tortillas

Directions:

Ask an adult for help. Wash the tomatoes, cut them into small cubes, and set aside. Chop the onion and ½ jalapeño finely. Add them to a large pot with the olive oil and cook on a stove top on medium for 1-2 minutes. Then add the chopped tomatoes and a pinch of salt, and cook on a stove top for another 5 minutes. Slowly add the chicken broth, stir, and cook for another 10 minutes. As soon as the tomatoes are soft, take off the stove and use a blender to puree the soup until smooth. Let it cool down and serve with corn tortillas.

A Tour of
Chichén Itzá

After lunch, we all headed outside. "I will take you on a tour of Chichén Itzá and show you where I found the TREASURE," Oscar said. "Maybe we'll find some **clues** about what happened to Thea and the NECKLACE."

We all headed down the path. But suddenly, Oscar's phone flashed with notifications. "Oh, excuse me," he said. "I need to take care of this. But the path is clearly marked — you go ahead and I'll catch up with you."

> **CHICHÉN ITZÁ**
>
> The Chichén Itzá archaeological site is in the northern Yucatán Peninsula. The Maya ruins cover about 1.2 square miles. In 1988, UNESCO declared it a World Heritage Site.

"You got it, Oscar," Computer said. "I will take care of these cheddarheads!"

Poirat looked up and noticed a long line of tourists outside the ticket office. "Walk FASTER. The line to buy tickets is enormouse!"

Computer beeped happily. "Don't be such a worryrat! I already bought the tickets!"

Poirat patted the computer. "Well done! You've been such a help with this trip. You should leave this stinky old cheese, Geronimo, and come to work for me!" he said.

"No!" Bruce Hyena cried. "You should come work for me to help plan my adventure trips. You would get to travel the world."

Squeak! Everymouse was trying to steal my computer!

Computer let out a few quick beeps. "It's

impawssible for me to work for any other rodent. My inventor, Beaker Poirat, built me especially for Geronimo. The two of you will have to get your own supersmart computer!"

Computer was sometimes **annoying**, but he was also very helpful. I was glad to have him.

As we entered the site, a sudden view of

We don't have to wait in line?

What a fabumouse picture!

TICKET PURCHASE LINE ONLY. E-TICKET HOLDERS MOVE TO THE SIDE. →

the central pyramid took my breath away. It was incredimouse!

On the land surrounding the pyramid was the ruins of an old town made of STONE.

"This is mousetacular!" I said. "I see why Chichén Itzá is a UNESCO heritage site."

"Geronimo!" A familiar voice called my name. Oscar had finished the business on his

We're almost there!

It's so hot!

phone and was JOGGING to catch up with us. "I see you've gotten your first look at why this place is so **special**," he said. "Come, let me show you around."

Our first stop was the Kukulcán

Mousetacular!

Follow me!

Pyramid, also called El Castillo, which means "castle." This pyramid rose up right in the middle of the archaeological site. It had steep steps along its four sides, all the way to the top.

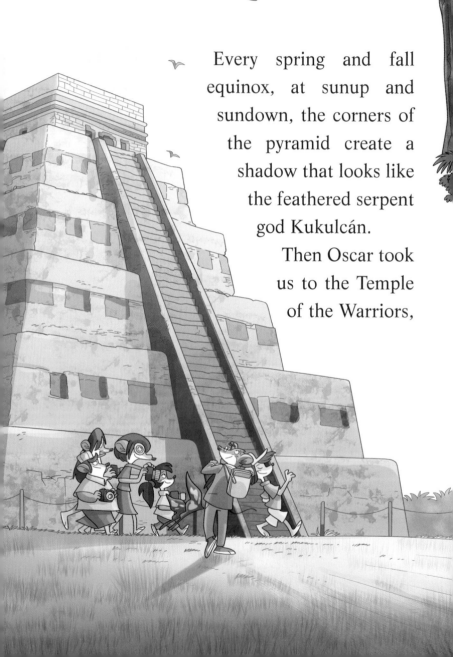

Every spring and fall equinox, at sunup and sundown, the corners of the pyramid create a shadow that looks like the feathered serpent god Kukulcán.

Then Oscar took us to the Temple of the Warriors,

Here is the warriors' temple!

another pyramid with steep steps. "All of these columns in front of the pyramid are shaped like warriors, hence its name!"

Next, we went to a stone court, where the ancient Maya played a sacred ball game. They threw a ball inside a stone circle twisted like a serpent.

The Temple of the Jaguars stood next to

the court. It had an impressive throne in the shape of a jaguar. Then we all went to look at a building where the leaders of Chichén Itzá lived called *las monjas*.

After that, we came to the Caracol, whose name means "snail." This structure is called that because it has an internal staircase that spirals like a snail shell. The Maya used this structure as an observatory. Their astrologists worked on their complex calendar here.

Finally, we reached Akab Dzib, the House of Mysterious Writing, where we admired many untranslated writings.

At every stop, I flashed Thea's picture around to the tourists and guards, hoping some rodent would recognize her snout. But so far, none had.

One couple I asked didn't appreciate me photobombing their picture. *Squeak!*

Every once in a while Computer beeped unhappily. "I'm still picking up Thea's phone signal in the Mobile Mouseum. Are we sure she's not **hiding** somewhere there?"

"It's unlikely," I said, discouraged. "But we're not having much luck out here. And the sun is frying me like a mozzarella stick! Maybe we should return there."

The others agreed, so we made our way back to the Mobile Mouseum.

Where could Thea be??

TAKING ANOTHER LOOK

As soon as we walked in, Computer began beeping excitedly. "Thea's cell phone signal is very close! She must be near here!"

Oscar shook his snout sadly. "This isn't that big a space. I can't believe we would have missed her. And she would have heard us walking around. Why wouldn't she come out, then?"

Poirat stroked his whiskers thoughtfully. "Maybe her phone is hidden somewhere around here. If we find it, it might have some **clues** about where she's gone."

I perked up. That would be a helpful lead — **FINALLY**! "Let's look around! But this time for Thea's phone!"

We split up. Oscar headed to the kitchen area. I walked through to the guest rooms.

I poked around, but there wasn't much to see. Certainly no sign of a phone. What if Computer's theory wasn't so cheesebrained and there was an area of the Mobile Mouseum we hadn't explored yet? Deep in thought, I TRIPPED on the carpet, pitching forward into the locked door that led into the recording studio.

As I stood there, catching my breath, three short thumps shook the door. I could barely hear the noise they made, but the vibration under my paw was unmistakable.

I leaned in and listened closely: three short thumps . . . three long thumps . . . then three short again . . . That was a Morse code message! SOS — which is a call for help! Could it possibly be Thea??

I ran to get my friends: "Come quick! I heard an **SOS** in Morse code coming from the recording studio!"

Oscar, Bruce, and Poirat followed me back the way I had come. Together we all charged at the **LOCKED** door, hoping to bust it open.

CRASH!

The door flew open and we finally saw . . .

MY SISTER, THEA!

Thea crossed her paws across her chest and narrowed her eyes. "What took you

MORSE CODE

A	·—	J	·———	S	···	2	··———
B	—···	K	—·—	T	—	3	···——
C	—·—·	L	·—··	U	··—	4	····—
D	—··	M	——	V	···—	5	·····
E	·	N	—·	W	·——	6	—····
F	··—·	O	———	X	—··—	7	——···
G	——·	P	·——·	Y	—·——	8	———··
H	····	Q	——·—	Z	——··	9	————·
I	··	R	·—·	1	·————	0	—————

MORSE CODE (named after Samuel Morse, who invented it) is used to send messages over long distances. It is a code where the letters and numbers are replaced by signals (either of sound or light) of various length, called dots and dashes. The code for SOS is very simple: three short taps, three long taps, three short taps.

cheddarheads so long?" she cried.

"We did our best," Poirat said. "Aren't you happy to see us?"

"We're rescuing you!" Bruce said. "A thank-you might be nice."

"I'm happy to see you, but I never thought it would take you so long to figure out I was in the recording studio. The Mobile Mouseum is not that BIG."

Computer beeped happily at my side. "I don't want to say 'I told you so,' but —"

"Don't finish that sentence," I WARNED him.

Thea's snout broke into a grin. "All right, bring it in for a hug, you stinky cheeses, and I'll tell you my story!"

I rushed to give Thea a hug, as did everymouse else.

"I knew all along you were here in the

Mobile Mouseum," Computer told Thea.

She **WINKED** at him. "I'm glad Geronimo brought you along. Without you, I could have been stuck in here forever!"

I groaned. "I'm the one who figured out her Morse code, you know."

Oscar twisted his paws together. "I'm so glad to see you are safe. I can't believe you disappeared right under my whiskers!"

Thea patted his shoulder. "It's not your fault. A strange rodent shoved me in here and locked the door from the outside. I YELLED a bunch, but I soon realized that with all the soundproofing, no one could hear me!"

"Who was it? Did you recognize the rascally rat?" Oscar asked.

Thea shook her snout. "No, but I'll figure it out. And when I do, whoever locked me in here is going to be **very, very** sorry!"

I believed her! "We want to hear the whole story," I said. "But first let's get you out of this room and in front of some CHEESY snacks."

I couldn't believe it — we'd finally found Thea!

As we turned to leave the room, Oscar had a sudden realization. "Wait, if you're here, where is the NECKLACE?"

Thea grinned. "The goofy Gouda who locked me in here didn't realize I'd hidden it in the recording studio during the alarm confusion!" She pointed a paw toward a **gleaming** gold chest in the corner of the room.

Oscar dashed across the room and opened the chest. Inside was the most beautiful **GOLD** necklace with a large pendant shaped like the sun.

"Thank you so much, Thea. You foiled the would-be thief!"

"I have for now," Thea said. "But we need to figure out who this no-good **rat** is, so that we can **STOP** him before he tries again."

Thea led the way to Oscar's office, where

MAYA JEWELRY

Around the tenth century, the Maya started creating small objects made out of gold, silver, and copper. The Maya craftspeople used wax casting to produce small metallic objects. They would create a wax sample of an object, which would then be used to produce a clay mold. Once the clay mold was made, they would pour metal into it.

she sat down at a computer. While he went to prepare her some food, Thea began to make a list of **clues** and observations.

"Start at the beginning, Thea, and tell us what happened," I urged. "I'm sure once we put all of our snouts together, we can figure out who's behind the attempted theft."

We must stop the thief!

Thea looked thoughtful. "My arrival here was mostly uneventful. But a few times, I felt like I was being followed. I could never be sure, though. That's why I sent that email to you, Geronimo. It seemed like I might need **HELP** soon."

"It's a good thing you did!" I squeaked.

Thea launched into the details of that day, and we were all **ears**.

THEA'S RECAP

1. Oscar and I walked into the safe room, where he got out the treasure for us to examine.

2. The fire alarm went off.

3. Oscar ran to get help. Even a small fire could be a disaster for the delicate artifacts. I grabbed the treasure and hid it in the recording studio.

4. As I came out of the studio, a strange rodent put a blindfold on my eyes and then pushed me back into the room.

This is what happened . . .

5. The door slammed shut behind me, and I heard the lock click.

6. I yelled for help, but no one could hear me. Then I switched to Morse code, and you finally found me!

A List of Clues

Once Thea had finished typing up her notes, she leaned back thoughtfully. "Obviously, the thief pulled the alarm to clear out the Mobile Mouseum. But when he saw I was still there, he pushed me in the studio so he could search the area."

"But you were in the room with the TREASURE the whole time! The joke was on him, I guess," Bruce Hyena said.

"Yes and no," Thea responded. "With both me and the TREASURE missing, it must have looked like I was the one who had taken it!"

Oscar and I exchanged a glance. "Well, yes," Oscar admitted. "Some rodents thought that maybe you had taken it . . . but I knew that you would **NEVER** do that!"

"Don't be worryrats!" Computer said. "Now that you're all together, and I am here with my search capabilities, I am sure we will find this rotten Roquefort in no time!"

Thea smiled at Computer. "You're right, of course. Now that I'm out of that room, I'd like to search the entire mouseum. Maybe the rodent who was after the TREASURE

Fabric . . . and a button!

A pawprint!

left some kind of **clue** to his identity."

We started back at the recording studio. Thea pulled out her magnifying glass and carefully examined every inch of the hallway outside and the door leading in. "Aha!" she cried at last. She triumphantly held up a piece of **khaki** fabric with a button attached to it. "This doesn't belong to any of us, so it must belong to the intruder."

She went farther down the hallway and hovered over a **pawprint** on the carpet. We compared

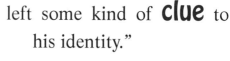
A compass!

it to our paws, but no one's was a match. This one was longer than any of ours. Near the pawprint was a small BLUE compass.

"I've never seen this before," Oscar said, examining it.

"The thief must have dropped it when he RUSHED down the hallway," Thea said thoughtfully.

Slowly, we made our way back to the office, so Thea could record our new **clues**.

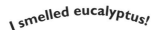

I smelled eucalyptus!

Then she tapped her snout. "Do you smell that? It's fading, but I'm certain I smelled eucalyptus."

Just then Computer made an urgent BEEPING sound. "I've been going through your records, Oscar, and I think we may have a problem on our paws. I compared your list of all the artifacts you should have here against all the pictures I've been taking. Lots of items are **missing**!"

"Oh no!" Oscar squeaked. "Everything should be here. We haven't loaned anything out recently!" He put his snout in his paws.

"Oscar, who has access to all your artifacts here?" Thea asked.

"Just me, really," Oscar said thoughtfully. "Well, and Manny, of course."

"Manny Chego!" we all squeaked together.

Thea stepped over to Computer and

1. Manny's khaki shirt is torn and missing a button.

2. The belt loop where Manny usually carries a compass is empty.

3. Manny's paws are long, just like the pawprint Thea found.

4. Some rodent stuck a piece of green gum on the fire-alarm button, to keep it on . . . it's green like the eucalyptus gum Manny likes to chew.

5. Thea smelled eucalyptus near the recording room.

1

IMG 58

2

IMG 60

3

IMG 59

4

IMG 61

5

IMG 62

started clicking through the photos he had taken. "Come look. I found **proof**!"

Computer really had **saved** the day. "Thanks for taking all those pictures, Computer," I said.

Computer glowed with **pride**.

"What do we do now?" Oscar asked. "I can't believe Manny has been stealing artifacts right out from under my snout the whole time we've been working together." He twisted his paws together **anxiously**. "We have to get them back!"

"We need a plan," Bruce said. "Manny is going to realize that we're onto him."

"You're right," Thea said. "He'll expect me to still be **locked** in the recording studio. I'll go there now with the necklace.

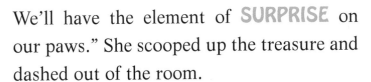

We'll have the element of SURPRISE on our paws." She scooped up the treasure and dashed out of the room.

Poirat leaned into Computer's screen to look at the photos again. "In these pictures, Manny is wearing a scarf with initials stitched on it," Hercule observed. "But the letters are *ER* instead of *MC*. I wonder why that is."

Just then the strong scent of eucalyptus wafted in through the office door.

Squeak! Manny had arrived already!

UNMASKING A RAT!

We all turned to look at the rodent **standing** in the doorway. He wore his orange scarf and carried a briefcase. Computer quickly closed the evidence window and pulled up my favorite computer game, *Cheese Hunt*.

"Oh, hello, Manny. Geronimo was just showing us how to master the Fondue Forest level," Oscar said **awkwardly**.

Manny smiled grimly. "You don't have to pretend. I heard everything. And you are correct, Poirat. *MC* are not my initials. My real name is Eucalyptus Rasmousen!"

He put the briefcase down, then quickly ripped a mask off his snout to reveal his true

Ha, ha, ha!

self: He was really blond and clean shaven, and he wore an EVIL smirk on his snout.

Eucalyptus sneered at me. "I think you know a rodent named the Shadow very well, don't you, Geronimo? You have run into her many times on Mouse Island, and you always end up looking like a cheddarhead. Ha, ha, ha!"

Eucalyptus opened his briefcase and our snouts dropped open in shock. Inside were

THE SHADOW

Mouse Island's most notorious thief. She's willing to do anything to get rich. She is loyal to Madame No, the evil owner of the EGO Company. Shadow is a master of disguise and has many tricks up her sleeve to avoid capture.

EUCALYPTUS RASMOUSEN

Unknown to everymouse until now, the Shadow has a brother who is a criminal just like her! Eucalyptus is a master con artist and an expert in stealing precious treasures from all over the world. He knows how to open all kinds of safes, how to pick any lock, and can disable alarm systems.

Like the Shadow, he is a master of disguise and can change his appearance to avoid capture. He only has one flaw: he likes to chew eucalyptus gum all the time, leaving that scent wherever he goes.

all the missing Mobile Mouseum artifacts.

"Those belong to the mouseum and the rodents of México! You can't take them!"

"Watch me," Eucalyptus growled.

"You're not going to get away with this," I hissed.

"I will because I have this," Eucalyptus said. He held up a small remote. "Over the last several weeks, I set up an elaborate sprinkler system in the Mobile Mouseum. With a push of a button, all your priceless artifacts, records, every piece of history in here will be destroyed."

Oscar let out a squeak and swayed in place. I put out a paw to steady him.

"Give me the NECKLACE, and I'll be on my way," Eucalyptus said.

"NEVER!" Thea yelled from behind him.

Eucalyptus turned as PALE as old

provolone. "How did you get out, Thea? I **locked** you in the recording studio!"

He stepped backward, holding the remote to the sprinklers in the air. Poirat seized the opportunity to reach out a paw and **TRIP** him.

Eucalyptus **tumbled** to the ground. The remote flew into a corner of the office and the briefcase landed with Oscar. Bruce Hyena seized Eucalyptus's paw.

"We've got you now!" I **cheered**.

But my excitement was short-lived.

Help!

The treasure!

Eucalyptus twisted his paw out of Bruce's grasp and quickly somersaulted toward an open window. As he climbed out, we heard the roar of an engine.

I sprinted over to the window in time to see a blonde mouse glaring at me from a fancy helicopter.

"The Shadow!" I cried. "She's here in Madame No's helicopter!"

We all RUSHED outside to get a better look.

Eucalyptus hopped on the

MADAME NO

Madame No is the CEO of EGO (Enormously Gigantic Organization) Company, a powerful company that handles deals all over Mouse Island. They develop shopping malls and skyscrapers. They also own airlines, newspapers, and TV stations. You don't say no to Madame No!

helicopter and it zoomed up into the air.

"See you around, Stiltons!" the Shadow shouted.

"Madame No brought her helicopter to pick up Eucalyptus!" Bruce cried.

"Does that mean what I think it means?" I wondered.

"Yes, you silly Swiss cheese," Poirat said. "Madame No is behind all of this!"

I shook my paw up at the retreating helicopter. How dare they! These artifacts belonged here in México.

Thea raised the Maya necklace in the air. It glinted in the light. "But the Maya necklace is safe and sound, and so are the other artifacts she tried to have Eucalyptus steal."

"Thea is right," Computer said. "We all made them look like real cheddarheads!"

THE MAYA
ADVENTURE!

Once we had unmasked Eucalyptus as the thief he was, Thea and I enjoyed a few days in México seeing the sights and prepping materials for an article we were planning about our experience. She took lots of **photos** and I interviewed local experts.

The trip to México had been **incredimouse**! But after a week, I was ready to go home and sleep in my own bed. Computer booked us tickets, we said good-bye to Oscar, and we **FLEW** home.

A few months later, I was sitting in my office putting

the finishing touches on my latest book. (The book you're holding in your paws right now!)

The phone rang and I frowned. I hate to be disturbed when I'm working. But I saw that my cousin Trap was the one calling and I knew I couldn't ignore it. He'd just keep calling until I picked up!

"Hello," I said. "You have to make it quick. I have a lot of CHEESE on my plate right now."

"Don't be a cranky casserole! I'm calling to invite you to dinner tonight at my new restaurant. It's opening night and you have to be here. Eight o'clock at Fourteen Robiola Road. Get ready for a FABUMOUSE surprise!"

Don't be late!

"What kind of surprise?" I asked. "You know I don't like surprises."

But Trap had already hung up. *Squeak!* I guess I was going!

That night, I hurried to the address Trap had given me. I gasped when I saw the name of the restaurant:

Just then the door flew open, and who dashed out to greet me? Why, Oscar Raton!

"Welcome, Geronimo, to my newest adventure: being head **CHEF** at Trap's newest restaurant!" Oscar said.

My snout dropped open in SURPRISE. "What! But how did this happen?" I asked.

"Poirat heard Trap wanted to open a new restaurant, and he remembered that I wanted to try being a chef. So, he suggested we could work together," Oscar explained.

"We kept it a secret to SURPRISE you," Trap said. "Are you SURPRISED?"

"I am!" I squeaked. "But what about the Mobile Mouseum?"

"A colleague is taking care of it for me while I'm working with Trap. But enough chitchat! Let's go eat some food!"

I rubbed my belly with a paw. I was starving!

As we walked inside, I could hear MUSIC playing and rodents laughing. In the dining room, I spotted Bruce Hyena, Hercule Poirat, Thea — and even Computer!

of good music, good food, and good friends.
What more could a rodent ask for?

Yours,

Geronimo Stilton!

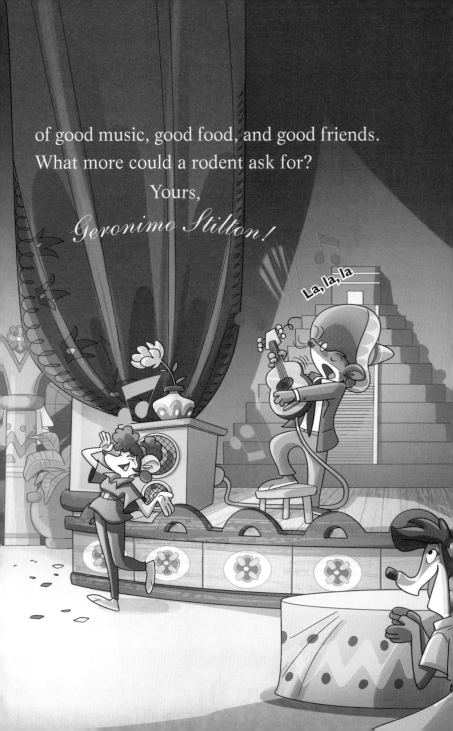

Don't miss a single fabumouse adventure!

Don't miss any of my adventures in the Kingdom of Fantasy!

THE KINGDOM OF FANTASY

THE QUEST FOR PARADISE:
THE RETURN TO THE KINGDOM OF FANTASY

THE AMAZING VOYAGE:
THE THIRD ADVENTURE IN THE KINGDOM OF FANTASY

THE DRAGON PROPHECY:
THE FOURTH ADVENTURE IN THE KINGDOM OF FANTASY

THE VOLCANO OF FIRE:
THE FIFTH ADVENTURE IN THE KINGDOM OF FANTASY

THE SEARCH FOR TREASURE:
THE SIXTH ADVENTURE IN THE KINGDOM OF FANTASY

THE ENCHANTED CHARMS:
THE SEVENTH ADVENTURE IN THE KINGDOM OF FANTASY

THE PHOENIX OF DESTINY:
AN EPIC KINGDOM OF FANTASY ADVENTURE

THE HOUR OF MAGIC:
THE EIGHTH ADVENTURE IN THE KINGDOM OF FANTASY

THE WIZARD'S WAND:
THE NINTH ADVENTURE IN THE KINGDOM OF FANTASY

THE SHIP OF SECRETS:
THE TENTH ADVENTURE IN THE KINGDOM OF FANTASY

THE DRAGON OF FORTUNE:
AN EPIC KINGDOM OF FANTASY ADVENTURE

THE GUARDIAN OF THE REALM:
THE ELEVENTH ADVENTURE IN THE KINGDOM OF FANTASY

THE ISLAND OF DRAGONS:
THE TWELFTH ADVENTURE IN THE KINGDOM OF FANTASY

THE BATTLE FOR THE CRYSTAL CASTLE:
THE THIRTEENTH ADVENTURE IN THE KINGDOM OF FANTASY

THE KEEPERS OF THE EMPIRE:
THE FOURTEENTH ADVENTURE IN THE KINGDOM OF FANTASY

THE GOLDEN KEY
THE FIFTEENTH ADVENTURE IN THE KINGDOM OF FANTASY

THE TREASURES OF THE KINGDOM:
THE SIXTEENTH ADVENTURE IN THE KINGDOM OF FANTASY

Don't miss any of my fabumouse special editions!

THE JOURNEY TO ATLANTIS

THE SECRET OF THE FAIRIES

THE SECRET OF THE SNOW

THE CLOUD CASTLE

THE TREASURE OF THE SEA

THE LAND OF FLOWERS

THE SECRET OF THE CRYSTAL FAIRIES

THE DANCE OF THE STAR FAIRIES

THE MAGIC OF THE MIRROR

Don't miss any of these exciting Thea Sisters adventures!

Thea Stilton and the Dragon's Code

Thea Stilton and the Mountain of Fire

Thea Stilton and the Ghost of the Shipwreck

Thea Stilton and the Secret City

Thea Stilton and the Mystery in Paris

Thea Stilton and the Cherry Blossom Adventure

Thea Stilton and the Star Castaways

Thea Stilton: Big Trouble in the Big Apple

Thea Stilton and the Ice Treasure

Thea Stilton and the Secret of the Old Castle

Thea Stilton and the Blue Scarab Hunt

Thea Stilton and the Prince's Emerald

Thea Stilton and the Mystery on the Orient Express

Thea Stilton and the Dancing Shadows

Thea Stilton and the Legend of the Fire Flowers

Thea Stilton and the Spanish Dance Mission

Thea Stilton and the Journey to the Lion's Den

Thea Stilton and the Great Tulip Heist

Thea Stilton and the Chocolate Sabotage

Thea Stilton and the Missing Myth

Thea Stilton and the Lost Letters

Thea Stilton and the Tropical Treasure

Thea Stilton and the Hollywood Hoax

Thea Stilton and the Madagascar Madness

Thea Stilton and the Frozen Fiasco

Thea Stilton and the Venice Masquerade

Thea Stilton and the Niagara Splash

Thea Stilton and the Riddle of the Ruins

Thea Stilton and the Phantom of the Orchestra

Thea Stilton and the Black Forest Burglary

Thea Stilton and the Race for the Gold

Thea Stilton and the Rainforest Rescue

Thea Stilton and the American Dream

Thea Stilton and the Roman Holiday

Thea Stilton and the Fiesta in Mexico

Thea Stilton and the Cave of Stars

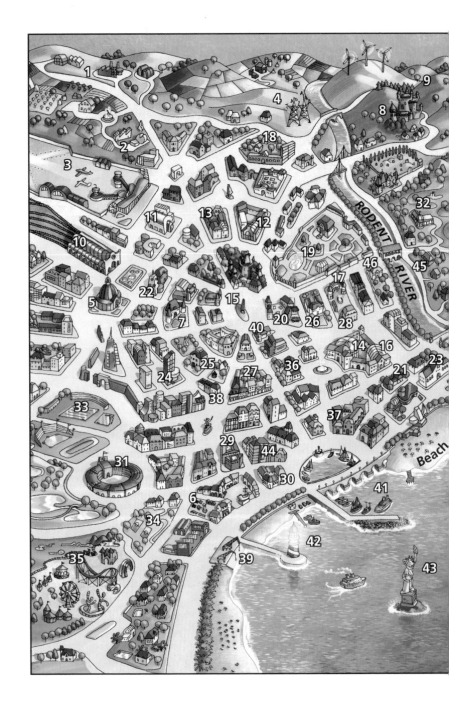

Map of New Mouse City

1. Industrial Zone
2. Cheese Factories
3. Angorat International Airport
4. WRAT Radio and Television Station
5. Cheese Market
6. Fish Market
7. Town Hall
8. Snotnose Castle
9. The Seven Hills of Mouse Island
10. Mouse Central Station
11. Trade Center
12. Movie Theater
13. Gym
14. Catnegie Hall
15. Singing Stone Plaza
16. The Gouda Theater
17. Grand Hotel
18. Mouse General Hospital
19. Botanical Gardens
20. Cheap Junk for Less (Trap's store)
21. Aunt Sweetfur and Benjamin's House
22. Museum of Modern Art
23. University and Library
24. *The Daily Rat*
25. *The Rodent's Gazette*
26. Trap's House
27. Fashion District
28. The Mouse House Restaurant
29. Environmental Protection Center
30. Harbor Office
31. Mousidon Square Garden
32. Golf Course
33. Swimming Pool
34. Tennis Courts
35. Curlyfur Island Amusement Park
36. Geronimo's House
37. Historic District
38. Public Library
39. Shipyard
40. Thea's House
41. New Mouse Harbor
42. Luna Lighthouse
43. The Statue of Liberty
44. Hercule Poirat's Office
45. Petunia Pretty Paws's House
46. Grandfather William's House

Map of Mouse Island

Dear mouse friends,
Thanks for reading, and farewell
till the next book.
It'll be another whisker-licking-good
adventure, and that's a promise!

Geronimo Stilton